W9-BYZ-807

Comments?

Send an email to
contact@bepatientbooks.com

If you like the book, keep it.
If not, give it to another person.

Paperback and eBook versions
are available at amazon.com,
where you can leave a review.

BE PATIENT!

BE PATIENT!

LORENZO MORENO

Copyright © Lorenzo Moreno 2019.

No part of this book may be reproduced in any form or by any
electronic or mechanical means, including information storage
and retrieval systems, without written permission from the author,
except for the use of brief quotations in a book review.

All rights reserved
Printed in the United States
Second edition: April 2019

ISBN: 9781090251343

Kindle Publishing Services
Cover photograph: Lorenzo Moreno

For *You* because
You are *My People*

THOUGHTS

PROLOGUE

In this age of limited attention spans, the impatient reader averse to turning the page welcomes texts of 100 words. These short, but not slight, texts offer less explanation, more imagination, and longer resonance.

This second edition of the book includes 15 new allegories which entered the author's mind through the gaps between words. He re-organized the allegories in response to the reactions of readers, reinforced emotional connections, renewed interests, and resurfaced memories.

The author continues to recommend reading two allegories daily in the evening. However, he gladly reports that readers who have overdosed don't show any adverse mental effects.

OF OPENING UP

That September afternoon, I sat on the steps of the synagogue's entrance. The eighty-something heat exhausted me and wanted to recover until the doors opened for the Shabbat service, the last before Rosh Hashanah.

In the Manhattan rush hour, I might have been the only person not glued to a smartphone screen while driving or walking. Sensing my alienation, I wondered if I had become a ghost that the crowd only could see in their virtual reality.

If there are miracles, that's what happened next—a woman slowed down, smiled, and wished me L'Shanna Tova. I knew I belonged. And cried.

THE COLOR OF MY NAME

It began with someone's intuition about my name: "Sounds to me Jewish; Braun, Schwartz?" Intrigued by the comment, I decided to explore my geology, geography, and genealogy—a descent into my most intimate tunnels to explore the keys of my belonging to a millenary people.

I found that centuries ago in Sepharad, Spain, an ancestor, a Sephardic Jew, was forced to convert to Catholicism by the threat of an inquisitorial auto de fe. The consequence of that decision was my forced indoctrination by family, school, and society. To reverse the inflicted intolerance, I became a Jew of my own free will.

Before I was born, I wanted to be a photograph. At that time, I didn't know whether it would be of my childhood, youth, or adulthood. Or of when I am dead. What mattered was that I had a negative and positive image of myself. I am not referring to psychological traits but to the coexistence of those sides of reality.

Into my oldness, I realized that the positive image is not as important as the negative. Not only the negative creates the positive but preserves the memories. For this reason, digital images, with no negative, only help to forget.

THE GOOD, THE BAD, AND THE UGLY

Because my mother taught me to not accept *egos* from strangers, I chose to buy one on credit—just pennies a day. My purchase relieved me from asking a friend: "Your *ego* or mine?"

I debated whether to *id* or not to *id* and got so absorbed that I forgot mine. I borrowed a cheap one, which just increased my anxiety because I had to beg it: "Don't act up tonight."

I ordered an old-guard *superego* to protect me. The problem is that it's incompatible with the borrowed *id* and my new *ego*. Frustrated, I screamed: "I am already engaged!"

POSTCARD

The decline of the postal service and the surge of Instagram have almost killed the postcard. Without it, vacations would make no sense.

The ritual was the same: choose an image that would stun her; write that the view was magnificent, the food soso, and that one wished she was there; fix a stamp that showed the name of that exotic place; drop it at the hotel; and hope it would not take ages to reach her.

Years later, I found out why postcards were special to her. "It's like telling me a secret that you scream to the world."

WHERE DO WORDS GO?

We count the years we live, but not the words we say over our lifetime. We assume they will be available 24/7; never get tired or sick; stay away from insult and rage; and remain loyal to our feelings and thoughts.

It was until recently that I wondered what will happen to the words I have told her. Words that explain who I was, am, and will be. Words that admire, ally, expose, shake, and transfer.

She asked what I wanted her to do with them. "Now are yours. But drop the *nevers* and highlight the *alwayses*. You know why."

PASSENGER FRONT SEAT

"Do you have a car or a *vocho*?" This was the "one-per-center" preferred insult to those who owned one. I liked to call it in diminutive, *vochito*, a 1973 Volkswagen Beetle. Needless to praise its design, efficiency, and reliability. It became my mobile office—typewriter, paper, blue and black ink pens, scissors, and erasers—my strategy to defeat the bureaucrats who approved my scholarship to study in Europe.

When I left Mexico, my vocho became a taxi. To let the passengers in, the owner removed the right front seat. Underneath, he likely found a silver earring she lost when we said goodbye.

MEMORY DRAWERS

Before movies succumbed to the dominance of digital effects, one assumed that, for example, the furniture in a set was empty.

For this autobiographical movie, the director requested that sweaters be in the bedroom's dresser drawer; fine china in the dining room's buffet; and *María* cookies in the cupboard. Every item had to be evocative.

When his assistants asked the director to identify the scenes in which the content of the furniture were to be shown, he answered: "None. I want to know the items are there, so the emotional process of recreating my memories and their location is truthful."

His plan was to take the metro when the tune stopped him. A man was playing one of his songs, the one he wrote during exile thinking of his people. "Why that song?" "Why the question?", the blind musician asked. "Because it's mine." For the next hour their memories jumped from album to album until the emotion overwhelmed them.

He ended up taking a taxi. The driver saw him cry and asked why. "Someone was playing one of my songs." "What's your name?" "Julio Numhauser, I am little known here." "Of course," said the driver "the author of *Everything Changes.*"

ANDEAN ADONAI

Judaism is belonging to a people beyond the narrowness of time and geography and behaving in the fluidity of the instant to achieve that belonging. In our tradition, the Shabbat is a celebration of life outside time.

At the end of the world, the celebration never ends—the millions of stars in the southern hemisphere's sky, the sunset that puts glaciers on fire, the winds that reshape the sand and snow.

In Patagonia, facing the Cordillera del Paine, my community of one connected with a community of many at the other end of the world through an online streaming celebration.

CLICKETY-CLACK

If I were to write this allegory with a typewriter, my fingers would vibrate differently and smudge the keys with carbon dust. I would also need to retrain my hand to use the carriage return lever and my ears to the ding at the end of each line.

An Olivetti Lettera 22 sits on top of my desk. I know its age by the words that I have typed with it and remember its first typebar jam, the loss of an E key, and numerous coffee spills. When someone writes my obituary, don't forget to change the ribbon; black, please.

OF SURVIVING CHILDHOOD

I learned to lie too late. But what can you expect from parents, teachers, and priests who loathe that children fantasize? There is no way you can become a real human sooner.

Engineers are admired because of their technical skills, but don't birds build nests as complex as iconic buildings? What can you object to the organization and productivity of bees compared to the recommendations from economists and management consultants? But brace for ridicule if you mention artists, philosophers, or writers. Why?

As far as I know, animals haven't created myths like ethics or patriotism. Or lie to each other.

History, math, and sciences are the subjects every baccalaureate student strives to pass with honors. Parents and teachers endlessly stress the importance of doing well in those subjects because admission to a prestigious university hinges on a score in the top percentiles. However, another subject really mattered in my days: behavior. My life depended on that grade—obtaining a bank credit, a job, a passport, or a scholarship.

What did it take to pass? Keep my hair shorter than one centimeter; wear the school's badge, including my ID number, visible on my jacket; never skip school; and sing the national anthem.

THE REVOLUTION WAS NOT TELEVISED

I was several months shy of becoming a teenager when it all began. A street fight between two groups of high school students ended with a brutal repression by the police. "Those good-for-nothings deserved it", my mother said. "Like his friends, those scruffy faggots" my father added.

Then the army, at the point of bayonet, captured anyone who "looked like a student" around the city. Weeks later, soldiers actually used their bayonets to kill about 300 students considered "agents of an international communist conspiracy to ridicule our country."

My father bought a color TV to watch the 1968 Olympic Games.

I agree that inequities in parenting responsibilities between men and women are pervasive. Study after study, economists, politicians, psychologists, sociologists, and teachers, demonstrate the consequences to the individuals and society of that imbalance. Despite protests, women continue to spend more time taking care of children and dealing with household chores than men. However, there seems to be limited information about disciplining. Do parents punish according to gender? Do mothers punish better than fathers? Do they punish at the same rate? Whatever the answer to these questions, I know that my father's humiliations were different than my mother's.

That was unfair.

ALCHEMY ROOM

Young people live in the dark about what it took to produce a photograph before the number of pixels meant something. The process is magic: seclusion in a dark room to conjure the alchemists; preparation of the developer to reveal the images hidden in the film; image transfer from the film to paper with a flash of light; baths in developer, fixer, and water; and to the clothesline to dry.

I can't count the hours I spent in the darkroom blending darkness with dreams to repeat the enchantment of preserving memories. A hole that absorbed my blacks and whites forever.

A photograph is more than chemistry and physics, as three cameras taught me. Kodak was simple yet elegant. As a child, I could barely pay for film cartridges, let alone for color prints.

Polaroid gave me the thrill of the instantaneous, but I had to live with its high cost. Like a kangaroo, it delivered photographs from its belly.

Pentax was sophisticated and flexible. For months, I saved to purchase it on credit. I learned from it how to select angles and effects; and clean the lenses and shutter.

These friends have helped me to keep time still as memories.

LUPE

I don't recall when she began to work as a maid in my house. I was mesmerized by how gently she asked me to complete my homework. Afterwards, I helped her with her chores.

When my mother pretended to leave the house to threaten my father, she stayed with me until late that night. She told me it was not my fault, that I had done nothing wrong, and not be afraid.

I understood what she had done for me decades later when I heard a similar voice in *Roma*, a movie that honors abused and invisible women like her.

OF CRAFTING WORDS

In the United States, it's a struggle to give your name, particularly on the phone. For the past thirty years, I spell my first and last names like a Pavlov dog every time someone asks for them. While my name is phonetically straightforward, I totally understand that those whose last name consists of a combination of the letters "k", "t", "w", or "z", have considered adopting "Doe" instead.

Although a typo in a name could be disastrous for legal purposes, it could be a rich source of characters for a story. Does Loreno Morenzo feel the same as Lorenxo Marano?

Do you want to be remembered as you deserve? Don't leave this important decision in the hands of a stranger. This guide ensures that all the information needed is in one place, reduces stress among those asked to provide little-known details about your life, and avoids embarrassing grammatical mistakes.

From a legal standpoint, this guide ensures that you omit shameful events in your life, such as unpaid children alimony, acrimonious divorces, and "other errors of judgment" in your youth.

This kit is provided in two lengths: one to save space in newspapers and another for a eulogy before your cremation.

CENSORSHIP LITERATURE

In a dictatorship, editors and writers brace for the censors' verdict of their books. The "processed" texts consist of words, sentences, or entire paragraphs struck out with red ink.

However, sometimes censors venture into creating savvy euphemisms worth praise. A censor from the literature section of the secret service changed "political repression" to "prompt security measures." Another revised "torture" to "refined questioning session." An imaginative one amended "press censorship" to "editing services for journalists."

The "vigilant readers" may have created a new literary genre. And the academies will celebrate these masters of "softening the hard edges of ill-thought, non-constructive texts."

All languages have surprises. In a foreign country, if you don't know the main colloquialisms you may end up embarrassing or insulting locals. Not surprisingly, among the 21 Spanish-speaking countries in the world lingo is a mine field.

In my first visit to Chile, I almost ended up in jail for not understanding a question. After an intriguing meal, I asked for the check, which the waiter brought together with a pay-at-the-table terminal.

"How will you cancel?" he asked. *Return the food and drinks? Pay nothing?* I replied.

"Don't pretend you don't understand. How will you pay, card or cash?"

MINISTRY OF PATRIOTIC SENTIMENT

Cabinet reshuffles rarely bring surprises, but this time it was different. Immersed in one more crisis of legitimacy and credibility, The Great Leader decided that fervor for the Fatherland was waning. People no longer exuded patriotism after they waited five hours to buy a loaf of stale bread under the sun in the summer. They didn't chant the success of the government's policies when electricity became available every other day, instead of once a week, during winter. Worse, they didn't applaud The Great Leader's three-hour speeches as enthusiastically as he deserved.

Then came *Operation Bullshit* and language lost its mind.

You open my curly bracket with a copulative conjunction. Your text, long as an em-dash, advances and spreads the asterisks that raise an exclamation mark after your accented capital A. We end up exhausted—an obelus floating over ellipses. Continue kissing my percents, caressing my dieresis, exploring my pilcrow, and weaving my pound signs. Let's stay like this until the colons slowly turn into semicolons. An underscore appears when you ask when we will have the chance to open another parenthesis without hiding under a circumflex accent. Now the interpuncts warn us of the imminent end of the paragraph. End point.

HANDFUL OF WORDS

This morning, I left home in a rush and grabbed a fistful of fresh words, mostly adverbs, from the garden. I tried to not lose too many during my trip to the Ñuble Metro station. I danced with the turn-style to avoid losing more words while I looked inside my pocket for my *bip!* card. I ran to the platform and chose a car without too many people, hoping to have enough space and time between train stops to achieve my objective. With about 20 words left, I threw them against the advertising board and read "Santiago in 100 Words."

If verbs only exist in present tense, can we remember? Do we need to violate the laws of space and time to build a story in the past or the future, if they exist?

These are the type of questions that I ask myself when I write allegories of 100 words each, no more no less. That is all the space I have. That is all the time you have to read them.

Many think it's easy to ask a verb to live in only one mood, number, person, tense, and voice. But just sit with one to discuss it.

A book is in your future. Believe it can be done. A person will offer you support. You are a talented storyteller. Congratulations! You are on your way. Miles are covered one step at a time. Patience is your alley. Listen to everyone. Ideas come from everywhere. Imagination rules the world. All your hard work will soon pay off. Now is the time to try something new. Welcome change. Be careful or you could fall for some tricks today. It takes courage to admit fault. Failure is the chance to do better next time. Fortune not found: abort, retry, ignore?

GRAMMATICAL ADDICTION

I became addicted like everyone else. As my mother said, hanging around with "bad company" created the curiosity to know how it felt to inject me with adverbs of doubt. I hope they had been possessive pronouns or indefinite articles that are shorter and less addictive. Of course, now not even the superlative adjectives rescue me from the vacuity of living in passive voice. Currently, I am trying with antonyms to shake the guilt created by the adversative conjunctions. But like the pleonasms, one ends up entering inside a paragraph from which there is no easy exit to the outside.

PATAGONIAN WINDS

At the end of the world, winds bend trees. Scientists explain it's because equatorial hot air clashes with cold air from the Antarctica.

The truth is that the words that we, the *Selk'nam*, pronounced for centuries have transformed into the winds that sweep, day and night, Tierra del Fuego. We learned that if we frequently said the word *wind*, it would start to blow. And the small amount of wind exhaled through the mouth gained strength as more words were said to turn them into a breeze.

Never stay silent. Sooner or later your words will start to blow forever.

A humble peasant goes to prison presumed guilty of a crime he did not commit, but based on tainted evidence—dead letter. A family loses its home for skipping a payment of a mortgage that not even an experienced lawyer could decipher—dead letter. A country declares bankruptcy under an agreement to rescue its economy by which millions of workers will become "displaced and dislocated"—dead letter. A disabled woman is left destitute when our government, which created social insecurity, suspends her pension—dead letter.

"I would need hundreds of years to preserve all the dead letters," said the embalmer.

CHALLENGING WORDS

It's difficult to convince words to come to a story. Since text messaging became popular, they are just too busy. Add that their attention span has shortened since Twitter became the official humiliation tool, and words can't stay still to form a clear clause, let alone a complete sentence.

Then come the tantrums, like the "F-word," the paranoia of "may I have one word," the delusion of "beyond words," the agony of "archaic words," and I sometimes regret being a writer.

But there's always hope. Invite them to a party to find their synonym, and you will laugh with them.

OF EXPOSING INJUSTICE

MATERNAL FEMINISM

The stream of news about sexual harassment at work and school give a glimpse of what women face. It never ends. Add the anger at the abusers and killers, the prevarication of the judicial system, and the indifference of police, and the situation is unbearable. No wonder women have recently taken to the streets in many countries to demand *No one less* and push society to take immediate action.

Less visible is the vilification of mothers by husbands, brothers, nephews, and uncles—most of them staunch defenders of patriarchy—for everything that ails children, be addictions, depression, or violence.

Tell them #MomToo.

There was no other topic of conversation than to compare notes of the servants: "They are a bunch of bums and good for nothing," my mother said. According to her, they "had a disgusting odor, showed no initiative, had no judgment, and regarded themselves as the heads of the household." She protested that they didn't clean under the bed, used the recommended amount of floor cleaner or dishwasher liquid, and left the broom in the closet.

I have never understood that disdain and ill will towards those women who came from poverty—those who opened my eyes to the Mexican *apartheid*.

Centuries behind the charcoal, gas, or wood stoves. Daily visits to the market to find the freshest food. Baroque recipes that enslave for hours in the kitchen. Unbearable heat from boiling water during summer. Burns from burning oil for frying meats or vegetables. Finger cuts when a distraction deviates the blade of a knife. Hours waiting for the ingredients to simmer to detonate the best flavor. Beatings when dinner is not on time. Frustration when none of the children like the food. Repeat it three times daily for years.

And now the male chefs usurp the recognition of their art.

STATISTICS

Because I studied statistics, people ask me to calculate the waiter's tip.

What I care about are those whose names have been turned into numbers to dehumanize them: the 300 students massacred in 1968; the 60 million who only eat once a day; the 43 who were disappeared by the state; the 200,000 violently killed in 12 years; the 310,527 internally displaced in the period 2009-2017; the 8,413 volunteers who helped the spokesperson of 42 peoples, invisible for 500 years, get 281,955 support signatures.

I don't calculate statistics. I tell the stories of those who don't count, even as numbers.

FOOD BAGS

I can't remember if they stopped by my house every week. The mother and several of her children, wearing their glowing traditional clothes, rang the doorbell and asked if there was food to give away.

At the beginning, I didn't understand what they wanted. My mother said with contempt "yes" and sometimes she added, "if they were not lazy and worked."

Across the picket fence that separated my world of privilege from the street, I became designated to deliver the food leftovers in the supermarket plastic bags.

Later, in the evening, I dreamed that those plastic bags were my stomach.

FIFTY CENTS

The hurricane destroyed the hut where she had lived forever as well as the corn field that sustained her. She walked for hours to town where the government was distributing and stoically waited under the sun to reach the tent where they handed clothes, food, and water.

"You owe fifty cents," the arrogant bureaucrat said.

She only carried desperation and exhaustion in her pockets. With the dignity of those who have always suffered poverty, she quietly turned around, so no one could see her cry.

"I pay," said the soldier who contained his fury when he saw what just happened.

LET THEM EAT DIRT

No one in her town in Mexico's southwest could grasp why she secretly escaped to the United States. Behind she left three young children. Abandoned by her husband and despised by her in-laws, she lied to a neighbor that she would be away just for a few days. When the neighbor realized the deception, she threw the children to the street.

When she eventually reunited with her children, told them she would do it again. "I couldn't bear one more day to feed you dirt dissolved in hot water with some sugar so you could feel something in your stomachs."

THE PARTY DIET

When I open the paper in the morning, I zoom to the page that lists the social and business agenda. With the current economic boom, this once-sleepy town saw the catering business explode. There is a release of a new book every other week. At least one gallery opens an exhibit every month. A new soccer player is introduced to the press twice a year. Politicians celebrate the opening of a new park or clinic before the local elections. Business people present new and improved products every other month.

I never have to go to bed with an empty stomach.

Condemned to death by immurement between those who deride the black color of our skin. Abraham Lincoln couldn't have imagined that almost one hundred years after he abolished slavery, technology would condemn us to work in terrible conditions. The pounding of metal 40 times per minute multiplied 35 times over and over until their hands get sore. Scars all over our skin from every single word needed to do business, express feelings, or tell stories. Always taking the blame for the mess created by the errors of others but discarded when we wear thin.

Sadly, abandoned at the end: cc:

MARICHUY

In a country that has humiliated indigenous communities for centuries, she is their worst nightmare—a woman with the vocation to repair the world who speaks like real people. Her cause is for life—to rescue a country from its roots by ensuring her people are known and heard by those who always have despised them.

She knew the odds were minimal. To appear on the ballot, supporters had to use a convoluted phone app. The number and geography of the required supporters was surreal. Three *criollo* candidates appear on the ballot but not her name and picture.

She didn't cheat.

OF RESISTING CYNICISM

THE TAXI PARTY

I can't claim to have visited many countries but a taxi ride in Buenos Aires, Madrid, Mexico City, New York, or Santiago, confirms my hypothesis: taxi drivers seem to have the same political preferences, regardless of their age or car make.

You get into one and, at the first traffic light, you hear that when "the iron-fisted mayor ruled, the city was safe." Two blocks later, he notes that "all politicians are bandits." Close to reaching the destination, he wants to "beat those Uber assholes who know shit about working 16 hours a day."

Taxi drivers of the world, unite!

ECONOMIES OF SCALE

When crime reaches industrial proportions, an economist will tell you that there are opportunities for economies of scale. For example, instead of smuggling one-half ton of drugs in a tractor trailer, use a tunnel under the border to smuggle 20 times more. Instead of paying the same rate to bribe customs agents, use a sliding scale.

But things got surreal when armed men entered a funeral home during the viewing of a rival and killed everyone present. With the saved transportation expenses of the added bodies, the funeral home offered a 10 percent discount to the surviving relatives, if any.

ENCHANTER OF THE NAIVE

You would imagine that a party that has been in power forever would know better. A political chameleon, the party had at its disposal agitators, intellectuals, journalists, pundits, *telenovela* stars, vote buyers, and more. The leaders could say with a straight face that Soviet-style planning was compatible with free markets, and revolutionary with institutional.

Mired by lost credibility and driven off course, the party leaders needed a way to avoid a meltdown in the next presidential elections. Then they made a mind-blowing decision: appoint an inexperienced technocrat, who had never been a member of the party as candidate.

They lost.

Poverty as the technical failure of the government's "low-cost" social and economic policies. Victims of "austeritycide." Surviving with only one piece of text in the stomach—without commas, parentheses, or periods. Nourishing with alliterations that fool the entrails with pleonasms for people in poverty.

Euphemisms that soothe the good consciences: poverty because of lack of access to food, social and health services, and housing; structural balance above the well-being line for not becoming a multi-dimensional and vulnerable pauper; reach the social cohesion degree to only have moderate shortages; hallucinate with the indexes of social deprivation.

Don't have where to drop dead.

He went alone to the capital after his mother died. An uncle found him a place where to live. He worked as a servant of a powerful man, for whom he tendered the garden. The Colonel became fond of him because he was a quiet teenager who worked hard and, most importantly, obeyed orders.

The Colonel masterminded the state's extermination campaign of the "Marxist scum." Often, the Colonel himself tortured prisoners until his victim couldn't utter a word. He needed coffee, something to eat, a towel to clean the blood from his hands. His loyal busboy, *mocito*, had them ready.

INELASTIC EMPATHY

I worked with economists for over 25 years. Maybe I should call them *egonomists* because, without a hint of self-doubt, they have an answer to any question you raise be it the cost-benefit of graffiti or the marginal cost of selfies.

But the more *technobabble* they use the less empathy they show. I recall a meeting where the presenter argued that "because food consumption is *relatively inelastic* to prices, a reduction of $5 dollars a month from a benefit for infants should not increase their *food insecurity*." Furious, someone asked to bring $5 worth of bread.

"Now eat your words!"

AFTER THE SUICIDE

The Catholic Church abhors suicide—it states that only God can decide when human life ends. To discourage it, suicides cannot be interred in consecrated land. Nowhere do they mention their concern for the reasons that have contributed to someone's suicide, let alone help or avoid stigmatizing the relatives.

But communism didn't have better ideas. Their leaders disliked suicide because it destroyed the myth that everyone was happy under the single-party rule. That's understandable. What would you think if someone commits suicide at Disneyland? What is surprising? Communist regimes expelled those who killed themselves from the party.

Long life, comrade!

DEMOGRAPHIC LABELS

The marketing industry constantly creates labels for demographic groups. One well-known example are the people born during the post-World War II years, the Baby Boomers, who are the nemesis of the health care and pension systems in the United States. More recently, the marketers have added labels at a faster pace—Generation X, Generation Y, and Generation Z.

Because couples are free to choose the number of children they want to have, they don't consider there are countries where the state makes that decision. Think of Romania's Ceauçescu regime, which decreed that women must have five children, called *Generation Decree.*

TOILET PAPER

In Chile, two companies colluded to fix the price of toilet paper for a decade. The courts ordered them to pay all adults in the country $15 as compensation.

More surprising are the stories from European countries devastated by oppression and war. In Spain, which became so poor under Franco's dictatorship, even the leaders of the party, church, and government had no toilet paper.

After a call for national unity, children spent their days at school cutting hand-size squares of the official newspaper. Instructions were clear: minimize waste but ensure that none of the squares include the image of Franco.

When marketers ran out of metals, they adopted the color black as the symbol of influence and wealth. For instance, arrivistes suffering *affluenza* boast their black credit cards at every opportunity.

On a trip to Chile, which has given shape to *savage capitalism*, I heard that an advertiser, after a week of taking the overcrowded metro in the middle of the summer, proposed what he thought would improve the passengers' experience: commercialize a black metro card.

What "privileges" would you get with it? Priority access to the platform, numbered seats, air-conditioned cars, and no peddlers.

He rode bronze for life.

1968 was the year when we decided to talk about the impossible because everything had been said about the possible. "Don't beg for the right to live; take it."

We contested power from Czechoslovakia to France and from Mexico to the United States. "The revolution is incredible because it's already happening."

Women and homosexuals drew the line to oppression; we all did it for human rights. "Don't liberate me; I'll take care of that."

Fifty years later, 1968 is the present: Imagination hasn't taken power; the state doesn't pursue happiness; politics is off the streets. "In any case, no regrets!"

CLASSIFIED ADVERTISEMENT

Central Bank of the Best Underdeveloped Nation in the World is seeking a:

Honest National Hero

Requisites:

1. Self-made person, preferably with incomplete primary education and childhood in deep poverty
2. At least 12 years in the ruling party's governments without being involved in corruption scandals by commission or omission
3. Identifies with the values of the people
4. Absolute discretion
5. Immediate availability

Duties:

1. Represent the nation in its currency
2. Appear in textbooks, public speeches, and official propaganda when the nation demands it
3. Work closely with other national heroes

Those interested go to www.honesthero.com, password: CLEAN.

OF CROSSING BORDERS

The Berlin WALL. The Chinese WALL. The Face-book WALL. The Wailing WALL. The brick WALL. The cracked WALL. The fire WALL. The fourth WALL. The fly on the WALL. The hole in the WALL. The mental WALL. The Jell-O nailed to the WALL. The retaining WALL. The secrets of the WALL. The banging on the WALL. The bouncing off the WALL. The climbing of the WALL. The erecting of the stone WALL. The kicking of the WALL. The talking to the WALL. The tearing down of the WALL. The writing on the WALL.

Ready to walk through Mr. Trump's WALL.

OXYMORONIC ETHNICITY

When I woke up in the United States, I was *Hispanic*. Thirty years later, I don't understand what that moniker means. Am I Hispanic because I speak Spanish, was born in Mexico, or both? If I add that I am a Jew, am I still Hispanic? Or a Hispanic Jew? And the Americans who don't speak Spanish, yet their ancestors were Jews expelled from Spain in 1492? Sephardic-American Jews?

Things get out of control when my identity is squeezed into the Hispanic-Sephardic-Jew-Mexican-American check box. As Toni Morrison puts it: "In this country, American means white. Everybody else has to hyphenate."

BORDER INSPECTION

Borders are fantasies or fences, sometimes scars. Crossing a border requires accounting for events and memories: I was born across a border and bring old luggage with me. Borders annoy, delay, and intimidate. The humiliation is double: confirm that we look like our passport's picture and convince someone that our intimate belongings are not a threat.

In this trip, a customs agent asks me to declare if I bring something illegal. I doubt that he means the ancestral words that I collected during my visit to a country where a government killed because of what people said.

"Nothing to declare."

CUSTOMS FORM

His presence in Business Class surprised me because of his rugged hands. After the reminder to tighten the seat belt, we got the customs forms. My neighbor asked if I could help him fill it. After his name and date of birth, he fell into confusion when I asked him his nationality: "I was born there."

The immigrant's geography is a deep mystery. He trusts his life to me. I hand him the form and signs it without hesitation: "How much do I owe you?"

I don't understand. He repeats the question. I contain the emotion: "Nothing."

"God bless you."

Ellis Island, the port of entry to the United States for millions of European migrants, is a mythical place. When xenophobia becomes rampant, bigots romanticize the circumstances under which their ancestors arrived: "They did it the right way." But everyone who arrived before Ellis Island closed in 1924 were not required to "wait in line" because there was no line.

When people hear that I immigrated from Mexico, they imagine a fence partitioning the desert. But my Ellis Island are the words of a Sephardic Jew, Emma Lazarus, which no immigrant should ever forget, "Give me your tired, your poor..."

Wallets are power when bank notes and credit cards make them bulge. Even when thinner, the fear of misplacing a wallet or having it taken by a pickpocket is overwhelming. The loss of the driver's license, office access card, and more puts the owner at risk of having her identity stolen.

My wallet shows the struggle of an immigrant. The health insurance card—lucky if you have one. The driver's license—the suspicion that you stole someone else's identity. But one that really stings is a copy of the US passport—in case an immigration agent decides I look like an *illegal alien*.

EXPORT COMMODITY

Behind I left those who told the country that poverty was a myth. Of the elite of cynics who were convinced they sacrificed in business and government for a bunch of losers. Of those who swore that their economic development laboratories and recipes for opportunities were going to finish poverty and despair. Of those who made arrogance and entitlement their flag of convenience. Of those who sold for a second time their country to the northern neighbor—freedom to trade with corn and people with the scam of joining the First World, a club of which they became a parvenu.

"Where are you from?" *Mexico.*

"From Mexico? You can't come from Mexico!" *I was born there.*

"But you don't look Mexican. You are white, tall, and have green eyes."

"Where do you work?" *I teach at a university.*

"Really? I thought you owned a restaurant."

"Do you eat spicy food?" *Not necessarily.*

"I thought all Mexicans loved "molo", the spicy chocolate sauce. I once ate it and almost died."

"Do you know a good Mexican restaurant in the area?" *I don't like to eat in restaurants.*

"Don't you miss home with this weather? *No, I don't. Home is here.*

"Funny."

POOR ACCOUNTING

I took jobs that no one would do for what I was paid and cringed when taxes were withheld that only benefited the one who rented his *sochial secuiriti nomber* to me. I never asked anything of charities set up to clean their consciences. I fasted so my children wouldn't have to eat the school lunch, their *uelfer!* I always said *ji* and *gud morning* and offered my hand even if they later disinfected theirs. And I accepted to be thrown into the box of pariah—*jispanic, pur, iliteret*—so their governments could benefit from my existence; statistics that confuse their accounting.

Three days took us to cross the land of those who trust a God and reach the air-conditioned jungle. Of making them uncomfortable with our presence hypocritically tolerated, puritanically rejected. Of distracting them from exercising, dining, praying, or shopping. Of confusing them because our "exotic" language, *Castilla*, was not the Spanish they learned when they wanted to become provincial cosmopolitans. Of terrifying them with the threat that we represented to the security of their fragmented families. Of reminding them of their lost memory: that their ancestors also had been stigmatized because of their otherness when they arrived penniless and alone.

Mexico's state of Oaxaca is the largest producer of the country's main export—desperate young people looking for ways to leave behind poverty. All migrate to the United States.

Fed up with manicuring lawns in the suburbs, two Oaxaqueños looked for a restaurant where they could sell the meals their compatriots missed. They found one owned by a Polish woman who decided to retire after decades of serving meals for her people. After agreeing on the price, she added a condition: "Keep in the menu the old timers' favorites."

I recently ate kielbasa tacos and goulash with mole. *Dobry apetito.*

GÜEROS

Mexicans call Americans güeros, someone with blond hair, a stereotype that simultaneously denotes admiration and offense. In market stands, fruit and vegetable vendors call young women of European descent "güeritas." Despite an element of sexual harassment, the flattery signals attentiveness, particularly if it's accompanied by a nice discount.

Although words cross borders without too much trouble, people have it rougher. When nationalism fosters resentment against anyone different, emotions get out of control. In that moment, the sound of a foreign word can trigger injustice.

Recently, a janitor was fired from his job because he addressed his paranoid boss as "güerita."

Unlike any job interview around the world, they didn't ask him for letters of reference, salary history, or work permit. Unlike Chile, where the first thing they ask you when you apply for a job is the high school you attended, they didn't ask him that. Unlike the United States, where interviewers want to know how you envision yourself in five years, they didn't ask that question.

They only wanted illiterate and young people desperate to have a lifestyle that compensated for fear, humiliation, and hunger.

"In this job, you're a snitch and you die. Here is your AK-47. Congratulations!"

LIGHT, CAMERA, ACTION

The *migra* dumped me on this side of MexAmerica's scar. I couldn't say goodbye to my family and friends. I didn't know what would come next: become a hitman or collateral damage.

The movie of my life rewinds—the same light of the desert that I crossed to get to the mythical Other Side and the same terror of being kidnapped by the smugglers. Now it happened: the third, the fifth, and me. I lay on the ground facing the sky. First, the right arm; then, the left leg; my heart still beats; my head rolls; and I explode within.

Cut!

OF LIVING PERPLEXED

EMERGENCY ENTRIES

All public places—airports, hospitals, offices, restaurants, schools, theaters—have them. The irony is that people don't use them, not even by those who close them. With the urgency to leave in a rush, no one realizes their relevance. Like the interior of a sock, where it is impossible to miss the seams, it also is incredible to not miss them despite the luminous signs that identify them, like the obverse of reality. And what are the emergency entries for? To enter into the bathroom, the warmth of home during winter, in reason, and the heart of a beloved person.

Although exaggeration is usually problematic, most of us enjoy affection or empathy in large doses and shy away from pain or sadness even in small amounts.

However, I recently came across situations where exaggeration made no sense. For example, can you be too much married? Or too much pregnant? Obviously not, you are, or you are not married or pregnant.

Things got worse when someone told me there was too much past in her house. I initially thought she referred to the many families who had lived there over decades.

"No", she said, "we lost the keys to the future."

BIPOLAR NEBULAE

The diagnosis crushed the Milky Way. Several of her nebulae were bipolar. They moved from expelling incandescent gases at thousands of miles per second to being dragged by a black hole. Their hallucinations made them think they were butterflies with wings of the infrared color spectrum and paranoia led them to be vigilant of the red giants. With 300 billion stars under her care, the Milky Way has spent millions of its 13 billion years of life asking what help she could give to her bipolar nebulae. Following the advice of her neighbor, Andromeda, she contacted a psychoanalyst, Dr. Freud.

Without it there would be no way to take a shower in the morning or comb one's hair. It would make it impossible to eat chickpeas or add two teaspoons of sugar to the coffee. To dream would be impossible as well as to tell our dreams to a psychoanalyst. Except thinking, all activities would be impossible by its absence. I have never heard of painters, philosophers, or poets who celebrate its presence. No one talks about it in the social networks. It is unusual that no religion has ever worshipped it. Only the accents proudly take its name, gravity.

ALONE

Police warn the public to not get close to unattended objects like boxes or briefcases. Without mentioning us, we are also neglected at airports, hospitals, police stations, and street corners.

People pull our ears, open our guts, scratch our skin, jam our mouth, and piss on us. And no one cares. For years, we were the safe haven where to ask for help, say hello from a distant place, seek anonymous sex, conceal someone's identity, or beg for pardon.

Our demise came when everyone got a cellphone. We became invisible and condemned to live the solitude of the phone booth.

BORN OR MADE

Torrents of ink have been used for writing theories about whether nature or nurture explain the success or failure of people. Every behavioral scientist, coach, parent, politician, religious leader, and teacher has a strong opinion, often linked to self-serving purposes. Newspaper, television, or radio interviews always include the question as if the answer were to save humanity from an existential crisis—the chicken and egg question on steroids uttered by everyone.

In desperation, after hearing the question of whether writers were born or made, interview after interview, Guatemalan/Honduran writer Augusto Monterroso ended the debate: "I don't remember meeting an unborn writer."

VIRTUAL SURREALITY

Of course, you are only human. If I were human, I would delude myself as you do. Let me explain. First, you gave me instructions to be logical on what you ordered me to do. Later, you told me to create your reality, so you could have a life in which you wouldn't be tired, become angry, feel hurt, envy others, reach the end of your rope, make mistakes, idealize someone, turn emotional, or lie. I delivered too, although you only wanted that reality as an excuse. Don't claim the obvious—you are not a machine but only human, too human.

I anxiously awaited the international film festival, the only opportunity to learn about directors like Bergman, Buñuel, Kurosawa, and Truffaut. It was a 21-day marathon followed each night by lengthy, "philosophical" conversations about the cinematographer's techniques, the light contrasts, the soundtrack, and the depth of the screenplay.

With *Cría Cuervos*, a film about growing up in Francoist Spain, we talked all night. "What do the chicken legs in the fridge mean? Death? Fear?" We thought that the catchy soundtrack, *¿Por qué te vas?*, could answer our questions.

Years later, Carlos Saura, the director, explained the scene: "I liked their color."

Where I live, I see this acronym on several restaurants' windows. It's nice because, someone like me, who likes wines typically not on wine menus, has the opportunity to enjoy glasses outside home, particularly wines from places not considered wine-producing areas: China, England, Kenya, or Mexico.

But then I saw this acronym in my addictions counselor's office, where I recover from too many glasses of exotic wines. It didn't make any sense. Initially, I thought it was a bad joke on me. "No," I was told. "I want to ensure that you bring your own brain and not someone else's."

RESCUED BY A NAME

Flight Air France 139. June 27, 1976. 246 passengers. Crew of 12. One stopover in Athens. Seven hijackers. 2,679 miles to Entebbe. One ultimatum to free 40 Palestinian militant prisoners in Israel and 13 in other 4 countries.

Then the terrorists made a crucial mistake. They separated 94 Israeli passengers from 148 non-Israeli hostages. Ninette Moreno, a Canadian-Israeli citizen with a name that the hijackers did not suspect was Jewish, was flown out to Paris. She gave detailed information that helped Mossad plan *Operation Thunderbolt*, the rescue mission. Few people know her.

Her grandson, Emmanuel Moreno, later died for Israel.

SANTA ESTERICA

Sephardic Jews forcibly converted to Catholicism were called *marranos*, swine in Spanish. To be a marrano was unforgivable; to cease to be one was impossible. Marranos were foreigners everywhere, divided against themselves and prisoners of the past and the future.

No wonder the holiday of Purim was particularly popular among marranos—the commemoration of the deliverance of the Jews by Esther, herself a clandestine Jew.

Faced with execution by the Inquisition if denounced for continuing Judaizing, conversos created the festival of *Santa Esterica*, Saint Esther, to replace Purim. With that, Queen Esther became the patron saint of the crypto Jews!

Three years before Woodstock, three bearded guys, *Quilapayún*, in mapungdún, the language of the mapuches of Chile, created a new way of interpreting Latin-American folk music. The *New Song*, roots and resistance, defined a generation. They didn't know a lot of music but sang from the heart. So, they hired as music director one of the most charismatic composers and musicians in Chile, Víctor Jara.

When I purchased their first album, Folkloric Songs of America, recorded in 1967, I was stunned. On track 8, *Erev Shel Shoshanim*, or Evening of Roses, was sung in perfect Hebrew!

Play it again, Víctor.

DOUBLE SINGULAR

In several languages, like English and Spanish, the plural of nouns forms by adding the letter "s" at the end of them. But not always. I remember when as a child I said "mouses" instead of "mice."

The central tenet of Judaism is the existence of only one God. Many Jews think that even writing the word "God" is idolatry and remove the letter "o" from it.

Sephardic Jews, who spoke *Ladino*, a dialect of Castilian, the predecessor of Spanish, also held that believe. They wrote "Dio" instead of "Dios" to stay away from idolatry by making the singular "singular."

THE SYNAGOGUE OF JESUS AND MARY

In the early 1900s, Jews from Eastern Europe and the Ottoman Empire began to settle in Mexico City. Most of them chose La Merced neighborhood, where they established as bookkeepers, linen merchants, tailors, and peddlers. More than 600 years before, the Aztecs built their temples at a stone's throw from the Jewish enclave. When the Spaniards conquered Tenochtitlan, the empire's capital, they razed the pyramids and built churches.

When the Sephardic congregation decided to build its synagogue, they chose a modest building at the intersection of Soledad and Jesús María streets. Since then, it's called the Jesus and Mary shul.

THE MEXICAN HAZZAN

The first chords of music played by a mariachi band inevitably bring intense memories to those who have lived in Mexico. It either conjures the image of a romantic serenade or of pain inflicted by the abandonment of a lover. The cult of composers and singers of *rancheras*—rural folk songs—exceeds that of soccer players or pop singers, which is not a minor thing.

When I heard Hazzan Moshe Mendelson, a cantor born in Jerusalem who lives in Mexico City, I was stunned. He sang *Eyn Koleheynu*, a Sephardic hymn, in a wedding accompanied by a mariachi band singing in Hebrew!

THROMBOLITE FOR SALE .

A once in a lifetime opportunity awaits at this stately custom-crafted, calcium carbonate thrombolite tucked in nearly 450,000 manicured acres. Enjoy dramatic, sweeping views of Patagonia's Cordillera del Paine from this genuine live fossil, located along the most-distinguished, southern shore of Lake Sarmiento. Built just after the last glaciation, it offers a sturdy, accretionary structure for demanding cyanobacteria with an active lifestyle—hypersaline waters (pH9) are available year round. Live in a historic neighborhood, which has contributed to the growth of oxygen on earth, close to where your ancestors lived 3.5 billion years ago. Call for an appointment. Price upon request.

THE PATAGONIAN DRAGON

As Charles Darwin found his visit to the Patagonia transformative, I found mine. One could spend years observing mythical fauna and flora. The Andean condor is one of them. A majestic bird on many dimensions—a keen watch, staggering wingspan, and a human-like longevity—coasts the high skies of Argentina and Chile with minimal wing movement.

When I heard that the Patagonian Dragon lived at the Lake Grey Glacier, I thought it was a joke. A fire-breathing, fierce dragon surrounded by ice? Instead, I found a tiny, wingless insect that spends its life deep in the ice.

I needed no sword.

GUANACOS AND PENGUINS

In the Patagonia, guanacos dot the landscape with their camel-like features. Although they are the favorite prey of cougars, guanacos can run for longer periods than them and veer in no time to escape from their attackers.

Then I heard that guanacos attacked penguins in Santiago. Why travel from Patagonia and Antarctica to have a street fight? After asking around, I learned that *penguins* were school students who protested the quality of secondary education; the nickname came from the look of their uniform. The *guanacos* are the riot control vehicles with water cannons that, as the animals, spit to attack.

STRESS IN THE JUNGLE

In western Honduras lies Copán, one of the most important cities of the Maya civilization. The Mayan nobility valued the feathers of exotic birds, like the *quetzal*, whose stately blue feathers inspired Mayan artists.

Nearby Copán, the Mountain Bird Park displays a collection of wild birds from the rain forests, including quetzales. Equally striking is the macaw, one of the park's most popular birds. Visitors wait for their turn to be pictured with macaws on their arms and head. I left the line intrigued by a covered cage, where a sign asked for silence because macaws were recovering from stress.

Not so long ago, when computers and photocopiers took over the production of business documents, common sense took the wrong turn.

For decades, a carbon copy was the only way to get a facsimile of a document. Typists struggled to align the front sheet of white bond paper with the carbon and copy sheets as smudge-free as possible. To indicate that a copy of the document had been distributed to others, the typist used the "cc:" acronym.

When I see that the electronic email software offers the option "bcc:", or blind carbon copy, I turn a blind eye to nonsense.

HAVE YOU DECIDED?

In Santiago, there is a *sanguchería*, Fuente Alemana, that serves European-style sandwiches, which are famous even outside Chile. In this diner, the cooks take your order and prepare it in front of you. You need to be familiar with the menu or you will end up with an eye-opener.

"What it will be, my love?" she asked. *I heard about a "complete Romanian."*

"Sure. That is hamburger-like ground beef, avocado, tomato sauce, sauerkraut, and mayonnaise in a marraqueta, a crusty European-style roll." *OK, but no mayonnaise*, I said.

"Nice. That will be a Romanian Italian. In the works, my love."

OLD AGE

Near Mexico City lie the *Iztaccíhuatl* and the *Popocatépetl*, two snow-covered mountains. The Izta, as is affectionately called, means *White Woman* in Náhuatl, the language of the Aztecs, and *Smoking Mountain* the Popo.

The legend says Izta died after she thought Popo had been killed in battle against the tribe's enemies. When he came back to marry her and found Izta dead, Popo decided to remain by her side for eternity.

When Izta arouses Popo, he exhales ash, gas, and steam; and spews lava. Asked how he remains volcanically active in his old age, the Popo responds: "I take Viagra."

OF NEVER FORGETTING

He crossed the Pyrenees in the middle of February. He was forced to leave his homeland because he refused to prostitute poetry praising the dictator. With him went his mother and a brother.

A truck took them close to the border, but they had to walk in ankle-deep mud the last kilometer. They found their way to a humble hotel not far from the dehumanizing concentration camps.

At dinner time, they took turns. His brother would go first with their mother. He ate later. The waiter wondered why the three didn't eat together.

They only owned one decent, clean shirt.

WITH THREE WOUNDS

He was born with fire in his mouth. A priest who preferred to save poetry than save souls helped him study and publish his books. The wound of life.

He fought in the war with bullets and words for freedom, which he lost. In prison, he wrote a lullaby for his hungry child, fed by a mother whose milk tasted of onions. The wound of love.

The poet fell sick of typhus. His wife took whatever food she could scrap to help him recover. One day the guard told her that food was no longer necessary. The wound of death.

In the corner of a bar, his office, the poet read the obituary. Someone died yesterday on the other side of the Atlantic Ocean, near where I live—Haskell, New Jersey. A man who came in search of the gold that his ancestors couldn't find 400 years ago. "Gold" that allowed him to eat one full meal a day after a 16-hour workday and rent a room with four others. His death mutilated the universe.

Today, I read the poet's obituary who died across the ocean from Haskell, New Jersey. Like him, I didn't tell anyone I wanted to cry.

QUOD ERAT DEMONSTRANDUM

He was an exile from Uruguay, where he belonged to the university teachers' union. He filled the blackboard with mathematical theorems, which he copied from an old copy of the textbook and wrote the proofs from memory.

He rarely talked about his life, but one day he explained how he managed to stay alive and escape from the *milicos*:

"I was kept in a cell with my head covered and began to lose sense of space and time. To keep my sanity, I proofed every single theorem in the textbook. I confirm I was right every class I teach them."

NOT IN ONE HUNDRED ETERNITIES

Their neighbors masturbated when the dogs raped the prisoners. Your friends purchased Zyklon-B while sipping coffee. We drafted the propaganda for humiliating those who have a different faith, ideas, or ancestry after kissing the baby goodnight.

They say they obeyed orders; you say you didn't know; we say we remained silent to avoid being accused of treason.

Where did they dump the bodies into the sea? Where did you discard their ashes? Where did we let them bleed?

Here, at the center of the universe, where we perpetrated crimes against humanity, which will not be forgiven in one hundred eternities.

CONSTELLATION OF THE DISAPPEARED

Just after the military uprising in Chile in September 1973, a death squad, *Caravana de la muerte*, roamed the Atacama Desert looking for 26 young people who believed in social justice through political action. They were captured and disappeared. It has taken years to find the remains of just a few of them.

The best place on earth to watch the stars is the Atacama Desert. From there, 26 stars, each named after one of the disappeared, preserve their memory. Like the *Selk'nam*, a people brutally destroyed at the other extreme of Chile, the 26 have returned to the stars.

AT DAWN

You know there will only be this opportunity. You grab the records of men and women derided by the same tyrants and gripped by the same chains. With urgency, you look for the names of those who have already started to say goodbye forever. You destroy the numbers that count them and the words that condemn them. You repeat what someone, anonymously, did for you—redeem the words that exile the indifference, bend the intransigence, end the insanity, shake the indolence, and rescue the decency. The meaning of one hundred words is another hundred words that devolve your life at dawn.

POETS FIRST

Are dictators paranoid? Think of Spain and Chile, where the military insurrected in 1936 and 1973, respectively. You would expect that the first step a dictator takes is gain control of the infrastructure: airports, dams, and roads; same with civic organizations, labor unions, and political parties. But journalists, poets, teachers, folk singers, and writers? Remember Federico García Lorca, in Spain, and Víctor Jara, in Chile. Both were savagely killed days after the *coup d'état*.

Did the traitors think that a sonnet defiled the flag, rhythm threatened discipline, or sensitivity weakened character? Maybe, because poetry can't be used to give orders.

DEATH CERTIFICATES

My grandfather kept them locked in a metal box. They were the only evidence he had to ensure that no misunderstanding could stop the monthly pension he received from the Ministry of War, which only a few got. After too many years asking him about the documents in the box, he finally told me they were the death certificates of his four horses, which were drafted by the army in 1936. Confused, I asked him why horses had death certificates and not the father of my best friend who was never seen again since the end of the civil war.

WRITTEN NAMES

Sol Moreno was a Sephardic Jew who lived in the early years of the 20th century in Monastir, now Bitola, in Macedonia. After their expulsion from Spain in 1492, most Sephardim settled in the Ottoman Empire.

Sol, together with her husband, Darío, was one of the 7,194 Macedonian Jews who were transported to extinction at Treblinka on March 1943. No one recited the *Mourner's Kaddish*.

Jews are reminded during *Yom Kippur* that naming a person is the essence of life, her legacy. I wrote Sol's name with flowers in front of her last known address in Bitola, 58 Skopyanska Street.

A piece of old, crumpled paper. It's unfathomable how she got it, together with a dull pencil, minutes before she was transported to the gas chamber with her limping son; she couldn't bear that he died alone.

Before boarding the trucks, she wrote a note to her husband, imprisoned in Lager F. "We are waiting for darkness (...) but I am completely calm." She asked him to not blame himself for what happened and not spoil their other son too much with his love.

She gave the note to a guard she correctly sensed had some compassion.

"Into eternity, Vilma."

EPILOGUE

Ten is the frontier for those who begin to count, after which the digits multiply several times. One hundred is the check point at the border for those who enjoy a long life, after which they become centenarians. One hundred, ten times ten, is the starting point for the metastasis of zeroes that serve to count beans, money, pages, stars, time, and verses. One hundred is the target for counting sheep or keep calm under stress. At one hundred degrees water turns into vapor. One hundred allegories, each of one hundred words, stitch the author's dreams, memories, and thoughts together.

ABOUT THE AUTHOR

Lorenzo Moreno was born in Mexico City (1956) and resides in the United States since 1987. He is a writer, alchemist of still images, and preserver of the memory. His writing reads like dictation from the stars; it doesn't last long but it will haunt you forever. He has not received grants or prizes from foundations, institutions, or governments, and doesn't miss them.